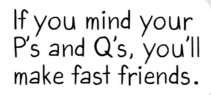

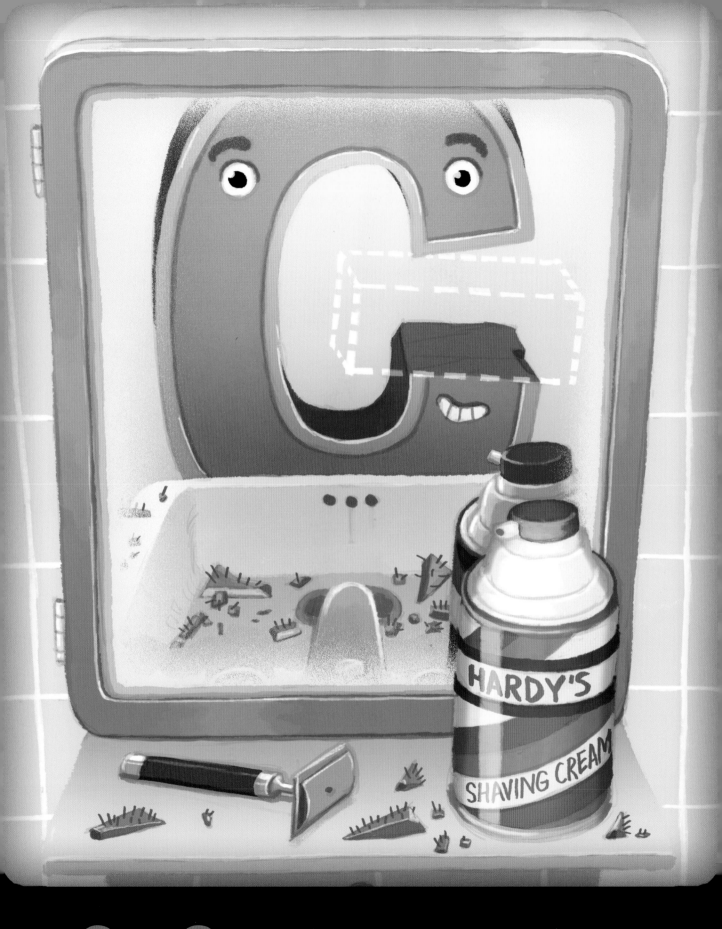

A C is a G with its mustache shaved clean.

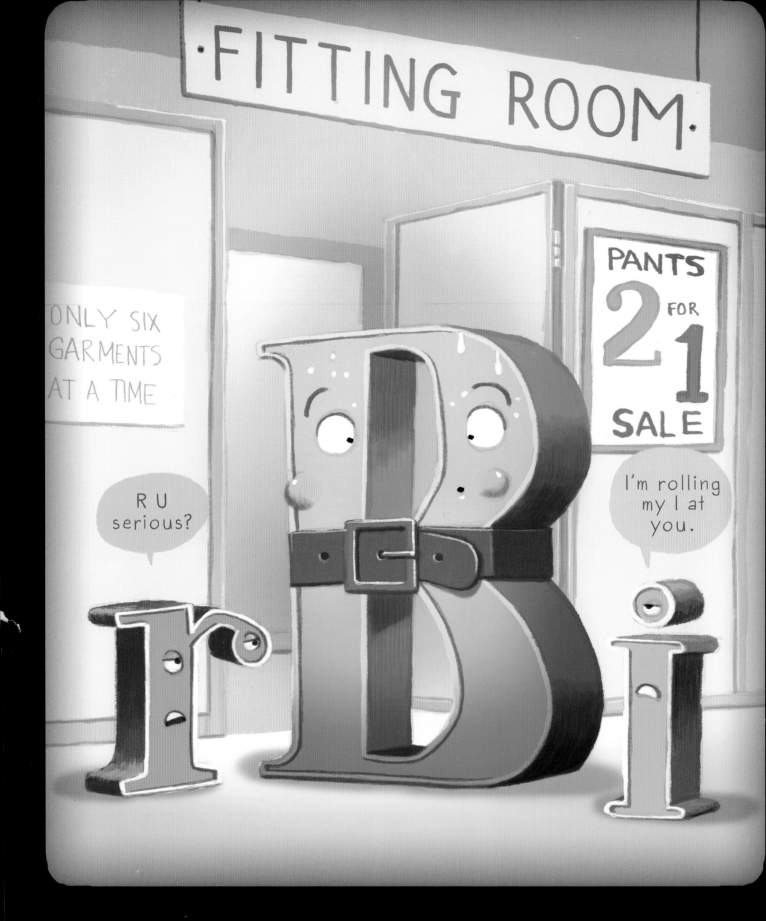

A B is a D with its belt on too tight.

An A is an H that just won't stand up right

Has anyone told you, "You look like your mother"?
Or, "You and your best friend resemble each other"?
When I was a boy and I heard that, I'd shriek:
"Can't I just look like myself? I'm unique!"

But all of us seem like our loved ones some days.
And sometimes it shows in the silliest ways:
The sound of our snoring. The shape of our toes.
The face that we make when we eat something gross...

We all look like family, so could it be true...
The alphabet's really a family too?
For all of the letters—from A on through Z—
Can look like each other in some way, to me...

An **E** is an **E** who on skis is quite fetching.

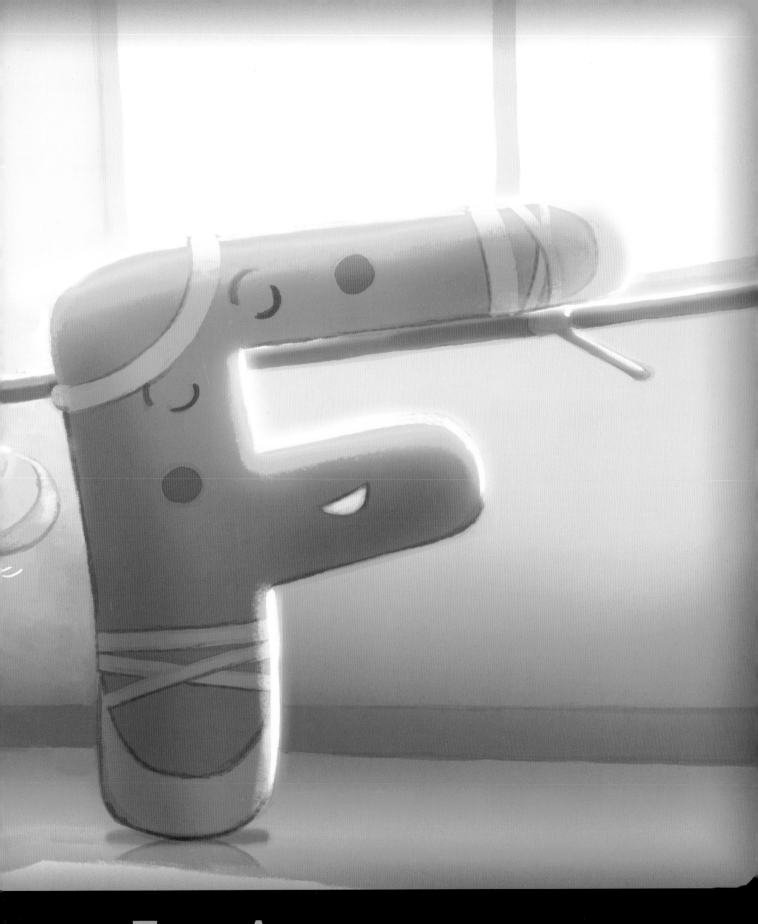

An **F** is an **A** with one leg up for stretching

A G is a Q that has started to yawn.

An H is a U with a pair of stilts on.

A K is a Y with its hat in its hand.

An L is an X waving "Help!" in quicksand.

An M is an N with a cane for support.

An L is an X waving "Help!" in quicksand.

A P is a B that just went on a diet.

A Q is an O that did not tie its laces.

An R is a K with a mask where its face is

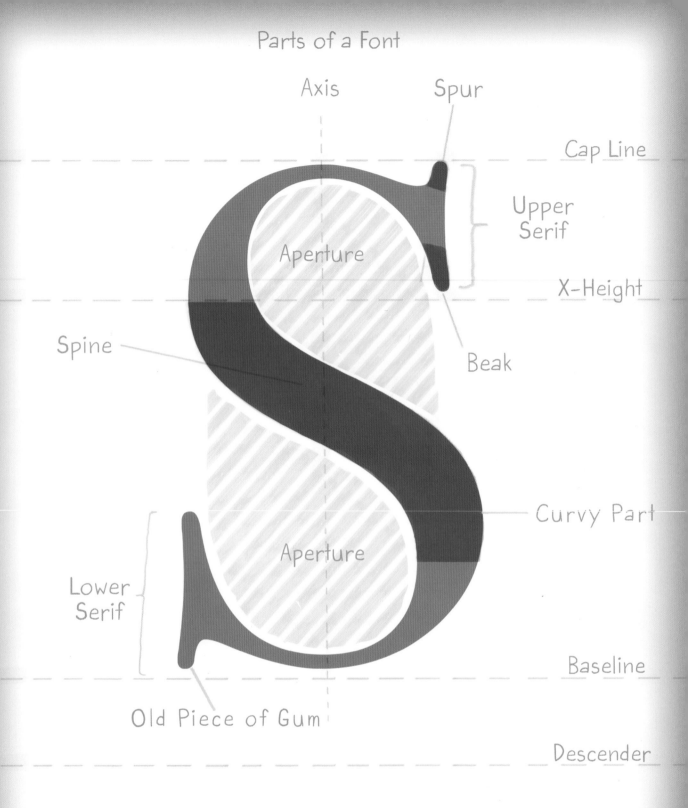

Parts of a Font

Axis

Spur

Cap Line

Upper
Serif

Aperture

X-Height

Spine

Beak

Curvy Part

Aperture

Lower
Serif

Baseline

Old Piece of Gum

Descender

An S is an S—it just is, and that's that.

A T is an I in a fancy new hat

A U is a J that's all slouched in a chair.

A V is an M that just cut its long hair

A W's an E lying down for a break.

An X is a V staring into a lake.

A Y is a T with its hair raised in fright.

And a Z is an L in a tug-of-war fight!

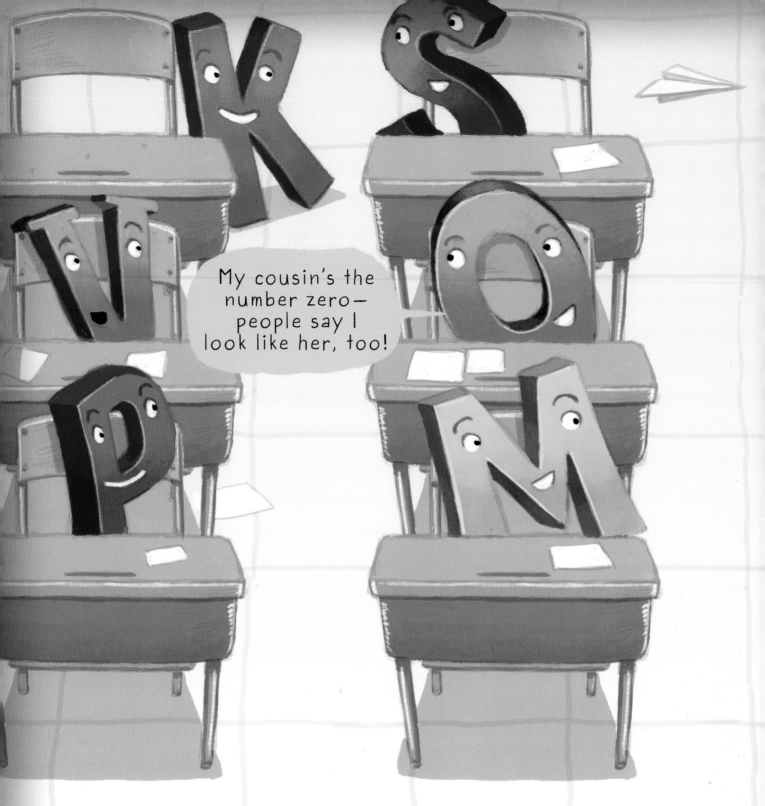

Twenty-six letters, unique from each other...
And yet, every letter looks just like another—
The same way that *we* are each special creations
And yet still resemble our friends and relations.

In those whom we love, bits of us are reflected,
Which helps to remind us that we're all connected.
I'm even connected to *you*. (I know, wow!)
The alphabet's alphabet makes it clear how:

IF **I** LOOKS LIKE **W**,

AND WE AGREE

THAT **W** ALSO LOOKS

SOMETHING LIKE  **E**,

AND **E** LOOKS LIKE **F**,

▷ AND THEN F LOOKS LIKE A,

AND A LOOKS LIKE H

(IN A RAMSHACKLE WAY),

AND H LOOKS LIKE U...

WELL, THEN IT SHOULD BE TRUE...

THAT AT LEAST JUST A LITTLE BIT....

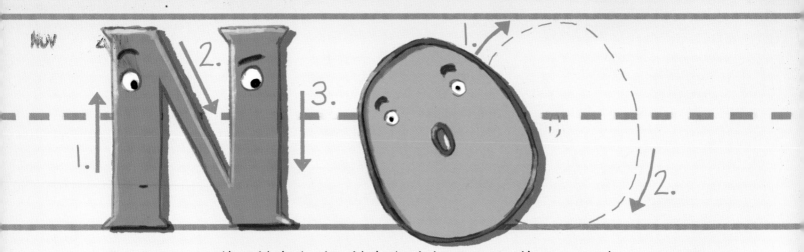

Can you use the Alphabet's Alphabet to decode this secret message?

IQI, KQH'DW DWFZZK SVFDY!

PHY OFM KQH BWOQBW YAW ZWYYWDS PWZQI YITOW YQ CWY YAW ETMFZ VWSSFCW?

EXEMYVO! RGA PYP YK! RGA EBI E SAUIBOIVYAS!

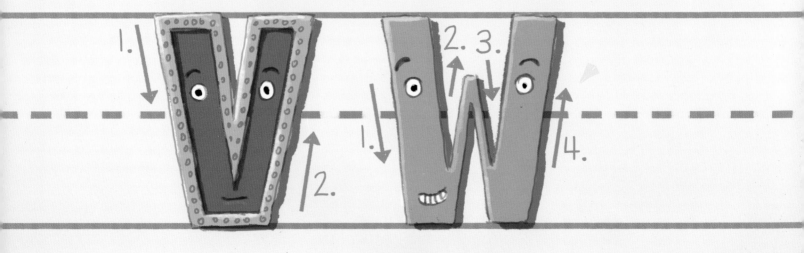